Swan Lake

Easy piano picture book

Music by Pyotr Ilyich Tchaikovsky
arranged by Alan Gout
Text by Catherine Storr
Illustrations by Dianne Jackson

Faber & Faber
in association with Faber Music Ltd

This book first published in 1987 by Faber & Faber Ltd
in association with Faber Music Ltd
3 Queen Square, London WC1N 3AU
Text © 1987 by Catherine Storr
Music © 1987 by Faber Music Ltd
Illustrations © 1987 by Dianne Jackson
Music drawn by Lincoln Castle Music
Typesetting by Goodfellow & Egan, Cambridge
Printed in England by The Thetford Press
All rights in music and text administered by
Faber Music Ltd, 3 Queen Square, London WC1N 3AU
Tel: 01-278 7436 Telex 299633

Also available:

The Snowman: Easy piano picture book

Music and words by Howard Blake
Illustrations by Dianne Jackson after Raymond Briggs
ISBN 0-571-10074-0 (paper) 0-571-10076-7 (cased)

British Library Cataloguing in Publication Data
Storr, Catherine
   Swan Lake: easy piano picture book
   I. Title   II. Jackson, Dianne
   823'.914 [J]   PZ7

ISBN 0-571-10077-5
ISBN 0-571-10078-3 Pbk

Swan Lake

A ballet

There was once a young prince, whose mother, the Queen, was very anxious that he should marry.

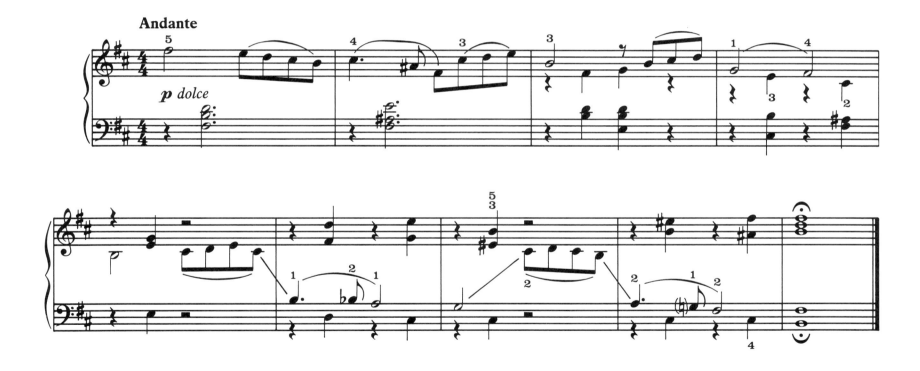

One day, when he was giving a
great feast to the peasants of
the kingdom, the Queen came,
with her courtiers, to tell him
that now he was old enough to
choose a bride. On the next day
she was going to give a grand
ball; all the beautiful girls of
the neighbourhood would be
there, and he must find one
whom he could love.

Prince Siegfried did not want to marry yet, but he promised that he would try to do as his mother asked. When she had left, he and his tutor went on drinking, and dancing with the peasant girls, sadly feeling that this was the end of their freedom.

Waltz

Tempo di valse

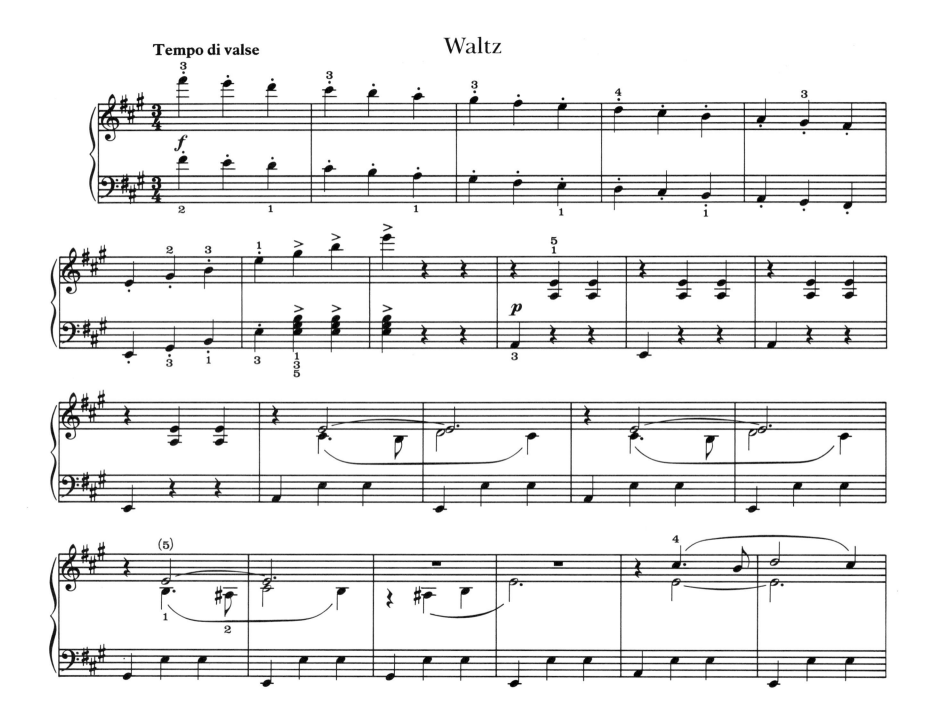

Suddenly the prince saw a flock of swans flying across the sky. 'Let's have a hunt!', cried his friends.
The prince seized his bow and arrows and ran after the swans.

The swans' flight took them away from the meadow into a wild forest surrounding a lake. As they reached the bank of the lake, the swans dropped their wings and feathers, and turned into a group of beautiful girls. One girl wore on her head a golden crown.

10

Just at this moment the prince and his archers reached the lakeside, and they drew their bows and prepared to shoot down the white figures which they still believed to be swans. But the crowned girl stepped forward and signed to Prince Siegfried not to shoot. 'Why have you come here with your bow and arrows? Why do you want to kill me and my companions?' she asked. 'Forgive me. I thought you were a flock of swans', replied the prince, thinking she was the most beautiful girl he had ever seen.

'In the daytime I and my maidens are swans; but really I am the princess Odette. A wicked enchanter cast a spell on me and my friends, and turned us into birds. It is only at night, when we fly to this hidden lake in the forest, that we can take our real shapes again', said the girl.

'Forgive me, princess. If I had known, I would never have tried to harm you', said the young prince. As a token of her forgiveness, the princess Odette and her companions danced with Siegfried and his archers on the grassy banks of the lake.

11

Waltz

Dance of the little swans

'Tomorrow I have to choose a bride. Come to the ball my mother is giving at the palace and I shall tell her that I love you and only you, and that I choose you as my future Queen', the prince said to Odette. But she shook her head sadly. 'I wish I could believe you. But the enchanter will never allow me to have such happiness. Before tomorrow evening is ended, you will have forgotten me, and have given your word to another girl.' The prince swore that he would never forget her, and that at the ball he would claim her as his only true love.

Pas de deux

But as he spoke, the dawn broke. The girls changed back into swans again and flew off, and from the forest came the dismal hoot of a great black owl.

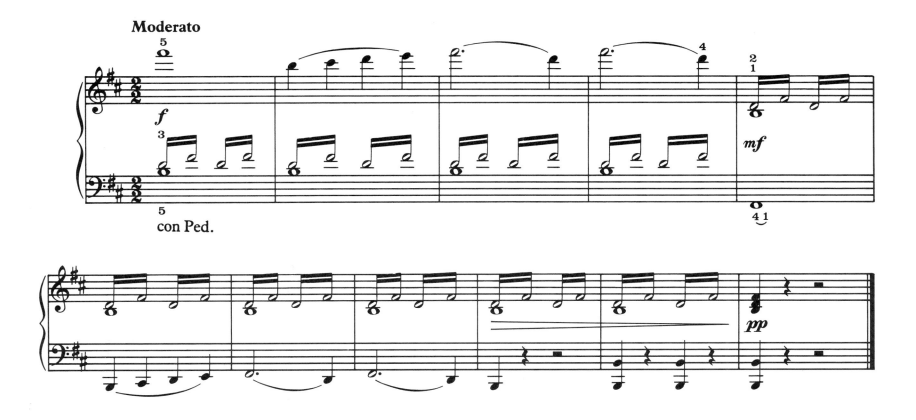

The ball that evening was as splendid as the old Queen could make it. There were hundreds of beautiful girls and handsome young men, and everyone waited impatiently to see which girl the prince would choose as his bride.

While they waited, they were entertained by dancers. First came a Spanish dance:

Spanish Dance

Allegro non troppo: tempo di bolero

then a Neapolitan dance:

Neapolitan Dance

Allegro moderato

and finally a Mazurka.

Mazurka

Suddenly the sound of trumpets announced the arrival of a strange guest, dressed in black, accompanied by his daughter Odile. Her father, the wicked enchanter, had used his magic arts to make her look just like Odette, and Prince Siegfried was deceived into thinking that this was the Swan Princess to whom he had given his pledge the night before. First he danced with her.

Pas de deux

Then he took her to his mother and told her that this was his chosen bride.

But as he did so, the cry of the owl was heard again, and the prince saw that his strange, dark guest had now appeared in his true form – as a demon – while the beautiful Odile no longer looked like the Swan princess, Odette.

27

In despair, the prince rushed out of the castle to search for his true love.

In the forest, the swan maidens were waiting for their princess.

Second dance of the little swans

When Odette arrived, she was in despair; the prince, her lover, had betrayed her, and had given his troth to Odile, the daughter of the wicked magician who had turned Odette into a swan.

The young prince had rushed into the forest to beg Odette's forgiveness. But just as he arrived, the demon appeared, and by his magic made the lake overflow its boundaries and threaten to drown the prince and the swan maidens. Prince Siegfried tore the crown off Odette's head and threw it into the lake. 'What does it matter to me that you are a princess?' he cried. 'For me, you are my beloved, and that is enough'.

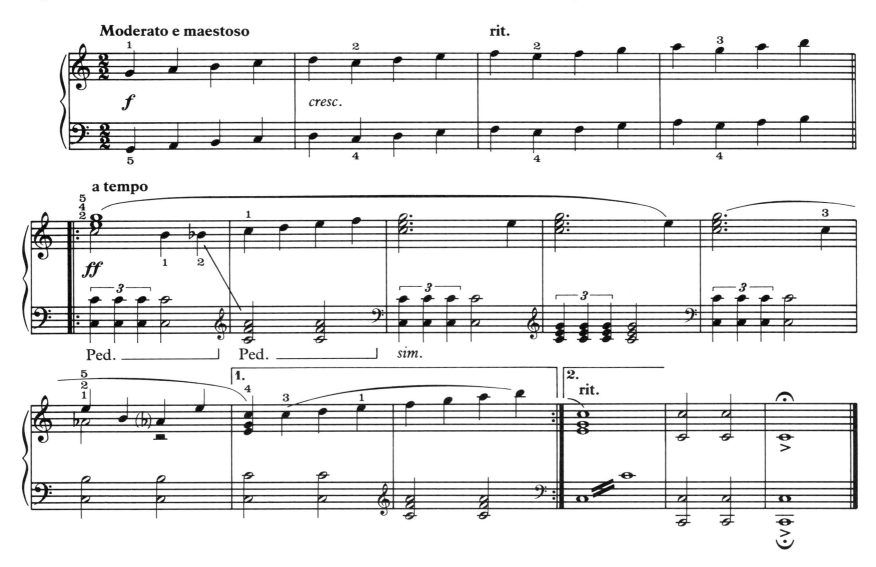

When he heard this cry of love, the wicked magician knew that he had no more power over the princess. From henceforth she would always keep her real form as a woman and would never again have to take the shape of a swan to haunt the Swan Lake.